D1157001

Ahoy, mateys! Do you want to join my pirate crew? Then just say the pirate password: "Yo-ho-ho!" As part of my crew, you'll need to learn the Never Land pirate pledge.

TODAY'S PIRATE PLEDGE

A Never Land pirate always helps out when someone's in trouble!

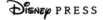Reader

WWW.ABDOPUBLISHING.COM

Reinforced library bound edition published in 2015 by Spotlight, a division of ABDO
PO Box 398166, Minneapolis, Minnesota 55439. Spotlight produces high-quality reinforced library
bound editions for schools and libraries. Published by agreement with Disney Enterprises, Inc.

Printed in the United States of America, North Mankato, Minnesota.
052014
072014

 **Disney PRESS**   THIS BOOK CONTAINS
RECYCLED MATERIALS

LIBRARY OF CONGRESS CATALOGING-IN-PUBLICATION DATA

This title was previously cataloged with the following information:

La Rose, Melinda.
Jake and the Neverland Pirates: Jake hatches a plan / written by Melinda La Rose ; illustrated by
Alan Batson.
   p. cm. -- (World of reading. Level Pre-1)
Summary: "Help Jake and the crew foil Hook in this egg-cellent adventure!"
1. Pirates--Juvenile fiction. 2. Eggs--Juvenile fiction. 3. Hummingbirds--Juvenile fiction. I. Batson,
Alan, ill. II. Title. III. Series. IV. Jake and the Never Land Pirates (Television program)
[E]--dc23

                                    2012289313

978-1-61479-246-8 (Reinforced Library Bound Edition)

Spotlight
A Division of ABDO
www.abdopublishing.com

JAKE HATCHES A PLAN

WRITTEN BY MELINDA LA ROSE

ILLUSTRATED BY ALAN BATSON

DISNEY PRESS

"Blast it!" cries  Captain Hook. "We've been looking for treasure all day, and we haven't found one speck of gold!"

A  falls on  head!
coconut   Hook's

"Do you see what I see?" asks .
Hook

"Is it ? That'd be the bump on
stars

your noggin, sir," says .
Smee

5

How many stars does Captain Hook see?

"No! It's a golden egg," says Hook.

"It's very pretty, sir," says Smee.

"Pretty? Who cares if it's pretty? It's treasure, and I want it!" says Hook.

 tries to climb the , but it's too tall!

Then  uses his plunger hook to scoop the  out of the !

7

On Pirate Island,  and his crew
are playing volleyball.
Woosh! The ball soars over Cubby's
head.

"Aw,  !" says  .
coconuts   Cubby

Just then, he hears something.

Hummmm. It's two  !
                   hummingbirds

How many purple flowers can you find?

"What's wrong?" asks  Jake.

"Hum, hum," say the hummingbirds.

"Crackers!" says Skully. "They lost

their egg!"

"What does your  egg look like?" asks Izzy.
"Hum, hum," says the mama hummingbird.
"It's the color of gold," says Skully.

" ?" says Jake. "I bet Hook thought it was treasure and took it!"

"Don't worry," says Izzy. "We'll find your egg."

 takes out his map. "Here's the .  has to go through Pea Pod Pass to get back to the beach!"

Cubby

tree

Hook

13

Can you find Rainbow River on the map?

"Careful, Cap'n. We're in Pea
Pod Pass!" says Smee.
"If you bump into a vine, giant
peas will fall on us!"

14

"Giant peas? Nonsense!" says .
Hook

15

How many vines do you see?

Just then,  Hook trips on a vine!

"See?" says Hook. "No falling peas."

"Cap'n, if you please," says Smee.

"Peas!"

Peas rain down on  and .
Hook   Smee
"Blast it!" cries .
Hook

"Stop these peas!" shouts .
Hook

"I'll save you, Cap'n," says .
Smee

"Whoa! It's  Hook and  Smee, but they don't have the  egg ," says  Izzy .

Do you see the golden egg?

"This calls for a bird's-eye view,"
says . "  , ahoy!"
Skully   Egg

"Great job!" says  . Just then,
Jake

the  starts to shake.
egg

"The  is about to hatch," says .

egg

Izzy

"We have to get it back to its ,

nest

fast!" says .

Jake

"This way!" calls .

Cubby

"There's the  nest ," says Cubby . "But how will we get the egg up there?"
"No problem!" says Izzy . "Let's fly!"

How many coconuts can you find?

 sprinkles pixie dust on the crew. They soar into the air! "Those puny pirates have my golden  !" says .

 Hook swings on a vine and tries to grab the 🥚 !
egg

BONK!

Another  falls onto  head.
coconut   Hook's

"Oh, look," says . "There are
Hook

those stars again, . Nighty-night."
Smee

"Just in time," says  Jake.
Crack! The egg starts
to hatch!

"Hum," say the 🐦🐦 .
hummingbirds

"Hum," says the baby 🐦 .
hummingbird

"Aww, he said his first word,"

says 👧 .
Izzy

"Hum, hum," says the papa 🐦 .
hummingbird

28

"You're welcome," says .

"Let's head back to Pirate Island!"

says .

How many pieces of shell can you see?

"Yo-ho, way to go, crew!" says  Jake. "A brave pirate always helps others in need."

"Today we earned some  gold doubloons for solving pirate problems," says Jake.

"Yay-hey, well done!" says .
Izzy

How many gold doubloons did we earn today?